Dress Maisy
Sticker Book

Lucy Cousins

Take the sticker pages out of the middle of this book.
Open the pages so the stickers and the pictures
in the book can be seen side by side.
Read the words on each page.
Children can choose which sticker to peel off
and where to put it in each picture.

WALKER BOOKS
AND SUBSIDIARIES
LONDON · BOSTON · SYDNEY · AUCKLAND

Find a vest to match
Maisy's best knickers.

Find dungarees to wear over her blue knickers.

Which animals live in the park?

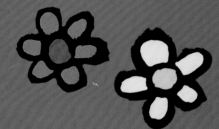

Find Maisy's pirate clothes.

Find Queen Maisy's crown.

Dress Maisy for the beach.

What else can
you see at
the beach?

Dress Maisy as a ballerina.

Dress Maisy for the rain.

Can you find Maisy's
blue painting smock?

And can you put another picture on her easel?

It's bedtime.
What can Maisy
see outside?

Can you find her pyjamas and her panda?

First published 1999 by Walker Books Ltd
87 Vauxhall Walk, London SE11 5HJ

11 13 15 17 19 20 18 16 14 12

© 1999 Lucy Cousins
Illustrated in the style of Lucy Cousins by King Rollo Films Ltd

Lucy Cousins font © 1999 Lucy Cousins

The moral rights of the author/illustrator have been asserted

"Maisy" Audio Visual Series produced by King Rollo Films for Universal Pictures International Visual Programming

Maisy™. Maisy is a registered trademark of Walker Books Ltd, London.

Printed in China

British Library Cataloguing in Publication Data:
a catalogue record for this book is
available from the British Library

ISBN 978-0-7445-6921-6

www.walker.co.uk